The Bunny Side of Easter

Story by Linda W. Rooks

Illustrations by Marilee Harrald-Pilz

The Bunny Side of Easter
Copyright © 2014 by Linda W. Rooks. All rights reserved.
First Print Edition: 2014

Illustrations by: Marilee Harrald-Pilz

For information on how to order the book, please go to bunnysideofeaster.com
Published by Papa's Press, 5415 Lake Howell Rd, Suite 171, Winter Park, FL 32792

A Note To Parents & Grandparents

On Easter morning, as we watch our children scurry about the yard, looking for Easter eggs, we may sometimes feel a disconnect between the legend of the Easter bunny and the real meaning of Easter. **The Bunny Side of Easter** fills the gap, taking children on an exciting and charming adventure with hints of allegory that point children to the true significance of Easter.

Christian sat on the steps, staring at his purple fingers and feeling gloomy. He had been scolded for spilling purple egg dye all over his little sister Audrey while dyeing Easter eggs.

He looked at his cousin Ryan.

"Why do I do things wrong?" he asked. "I'll never be good."

"You do lots of good things," Ryan said. "You're my best friend."

Christian rubbed his fingers trying to get the purple dye off.

"I want to be good."

He took a deep breath and stood up.
"I want to be a hero!"

"Me too!" Ryan said.

"That reminds me of the Easter Bunny," Ryan said.

"The Easter Bunny? Why?" asked Christian.

"Nana told me that before the Easter Bunny was the Easter Bunny, he was just a plain ordinary rabbit who didn't always do things right. Then he did something really, really good and became a hero."

"The Easter Bunny was a hero?"

"Yeah," Ryan said and pointed to the moon. It was the evening before Easter, and a bright round moon appeared over the rooftops of town.

"And now the Easter Bunny is up in that moon."

"Nah," Christian said.

"Yeah, I mean it. Look. Don't you see him up there? See his ears up at the top?"

Christian peered up at the glowing moon for a long time. "No, I don't . . . wait! Yes, I see him! How did he get up there?"

"Let's ask Nana to tell us the story," Ryan said.

They found Nana inside with the other cousins. She came back out with them. Audrey, Travis and Carson came too.

It was really dark now, almost bedtime, and the moon was rising higher in the sky.

"Let's sit here and look at the moon," Nana said, "and I'll tell you the story of how the Easter Bunny got up there. Two other animals are in the story too—a monkey and a duck. And there's also an angel."

Audrey's blond curls bobbed up and down. "An angel?"

Christian scrunched his eyes. "Is the monkey mean?"

"No, the monkey's a nice monkey, but there's also a tiger. And he's . . . well, I don't want to ruin the story," Nana said. "Shut your eyes and imagine you are in a far off land, a very long time ago, on the day before the first Easter. It happened like this."

Near a forest of tall trees waved a field of tall grass beside Farmer Flannigan's carrot patch. Down in the grass and up on top, long pointed ears popped up and down as a family of little brown bunnies hippity-hopped past the carrot patch.

But, little bunny Hal didn't hop past Farmer Flannigan's carrot patch like the other bunnies did because Hal liked . . . CARROTS!

Hal hopped to the fence, and read a sign that said:

This is mine! Any rabbit I catch stealing from my carrot patch will pay a fine. So every rabbit BEWARE! I watch my carrot patch with care.
Farmer Flannigan

Hal didn't care what the sign said. He hopped over the fence into the carrot patch and nibbled on the end of a carrot, then sang a happy tune.

"I love carrots for lunch and carrots by the bunch.

Carrots crunch, crunch, crunch as I munch, munch, munch,

on a crunchy, munchy bunch."

Hal gobbled up the carrot and listened to it crunch.

Suddenly, he heard another crunch—the crunch, crunch, crunch of Farmer Flannigan's boots!

Crunch. Crunch.

Frightened little Hal leaped over the fence. He hippity-hopped as fast as he could until he could hop no more. He stopped.

Where was he? He had never been there before.

He looked up.

He looked down.

He looked all around.

But all he could see were tall, tall trees. The trees began to fade into the darkness.

Hal's heart beat oh, so fast. Was this the forest?

The forest where the tiger roams?

Hal wanted to go home!

A whispering breeze brought the sound of crying through the trees. Hal cocked both ears. Was the crying near or far away? He hopped here. He hopped there.

And beneath a tree he saw a duck fast asleep.

Hal didn't make a peep. He hopped closer to the duck. Was the duck crying in his sleep? No, he didn't look like he was crying in his sleep.

What is this strange thing that cries, but doesn't cry? He sniffed and his ear tickled the duck's nose.

The duck awoke. "Oh!" said the startled duck.

"Oh!" said Hal, the curious bunny.

"Who are you?" asked the duck.

"I'm Hallelujah, but you can call me Hal. Who are you?"

"I'm Dasper," quacked the duck. "What are you doing here?"

"I heard someone crying, and it seemed loudest underneath this tree," said Hal.

"Crying? No one's crying here," said the duck.

"But, I hear it," said Hal.

"Oh! It's raining," said the duck. "I just felt a raindrop on my head."

"It's not raining," said the bunny, "but I hear someone crying."

"Yes, it's raining," said the duck. "Feel the drop of rain on my head."

The duck leaned down and the bunny felt the top of his head. To his surprise, there was a raindrop on his head.

They both looked up through the tree as far as they could see.

Splat! Little drops of wetness hit them in their faces.

Hal tasted the drop. "This isn't a raindrop. It's salty like a tear. I told you I heard someone crying. Someone's crying up in this tree."

They looked up through the top limbs of the tree where the moon appeared . . . a bright, round moon that made the night seem like noon.

"What do you see?" asked the bunny.

"I see something furry," said the duck.

"Is it a monkey?" asked the bunny.

"I think it is," said the duck.

Just then they saw another tear

FALLING

"Hellooo, hellooo," called the bunny and duck together.

A tiny voice answered from the top of the tree. "Who are you?"

"I'm Hallelujah, but you can call me Hal."

"I'm Dasper," quacked the duck.

"I'm Madeline and I can't get down," said the voice in the tree. "Can you get me down?" Then Madeline asked, "Who's that with you?"

"Who is who with who?" Hal and Dasper cried, looking at each other. "Where?"

"On the other side of that bush," Madeline said, "there's someone else there."

Dasper waddled around the bush to the left. Hal hippity-hopped around the bush to the right.

And behind the bush they found . . .

a little girl with wings sitting on the ground. She was a pretty little thing with blonde curls that hung in rings.

"Who are you?" asked Hal and Dasper.

"I'm Audrey."

"Are you a bird?" asked the duck.

"She looks more like a little girl," the bunny said.

"I'm an angel. I come from God," Audrey said.

"Can you fly?" asked the duck.

"Not very well yet." She frowned.

"Can you make a miracle?" asked the bunny.

"Every angel can make a miracle," Audrey said shyly, "with the help of God."

"Let's see one," said the duck, "and then I'll believe you're not a bird."

"Oh, no!" she said. "Angels do miracles to bring God's love from Heaven to Earth. Angels never use miracles just for play. The older angels teach us that every day."

Just then they heard a cry from up in the trees. "Won't somebody get me down? Please?"

"How'd you get up there?" Dasper called. "You look like a monkey. Can't you climb down?"

"I'm too small," Madeline cried. "Mommy and Daddy told me not to go so high. But I wanted to climb like the older monkeys did, and now I can't get down." Again, she began to cry.

"What can we do?" asked Hal.

"Not much," said the duck. "We're not big enough."

"You're never too small to do good," the angel said. "I know one big thing to do. We'll pray."

The animals got down on their knees and looked up through the trees.

Audrey began to pray.

"Oh me, oh my!" she cried, jumping up.

"Whatever could the matter be?" asked Hal and Dasper on their knees.

"I almost forgot. I don't think God can help me tonight."

"Why not?" Hal asked.

"Tomorrow God will do the most important miracle the world will ever know. God's son Jesus will rise from the dead and we will know forever He loves us so."

She flapped her wings, and rose up on her toes. "God loves us soooo much."

"How much?" Hal asked.

Audrey stretched her arms as wide as she could. "This much!"

"Wow, that's a lot," Hal said.

Dasper fluffed his tail. "But why can't He help the monkey tonight?"

The angel frowned. "I don't know, but I'm afraid to ask. Tonight He's busy getting ready, don't you see? How can I ask God to get a monkey down from a tree?"

"Then you do a miracle," Dasper said.

Audrey folded her wings and looked very gloomy. "I'm not strong enough to make a miracle without God's help. Something might go wrong if I try to do it by myself."

They could hear the monkey crying high up in the tree.

The bunny and duck didn't understand. Why couldn't an angel make a miracle by herself?

"I want to help." Audrey gave a sigh. "Okay, I'll try."

Audrey knelt down and folded her wings around a tiny wildflower on the ground. She closed her eyes and sang the song that angels sing so beautifully. The flower began to grow higher and higher, taller and taller, up through the leaves of the tree, up to the very top, up to the monkey, Madeline.

"Hooray," cried the bunny and duck together. "It's working!"

"Sit on the blossom," the angel told the monkey. "I'll bring you down to the ground."

Madeline sat on the blossom and held on tight to the golden rod in the middle.

The angel folded her wings around the stem of the flower and sang again the beautiful angel song. The flower began to shrink down through the leaves, lower and lower, until suddenly it stopped.

Then the angel spun around
and wilted like the flower on the ground.

Madeline the monkey sat up and looked around.

But the angel stayed lying on the ground
not making a sound.

"What's wrong?" asked Madeline.

"Angels aren't strong enough to make miracles without God's help," said Hal. "But, she tried it anyway all by herself."

"Is she dead?" asked Dasper.

"I think she's asleep," Hal said.

Madeline began to cry.

"She did it just for me! If I'd listened to Mommy and Daddy,

I wouldn't have gone so high up in the tree,

and the angel would be all right.

Oh, this is such a scary night!"

"I'm not asleep. I'm just so weak . . ." the angel said and she began to weep.

"She needs food," said Hal, rubbing his tummy. "My mommy says food makes strong bunnies."

"Are angels like bunnies?" Dasper asked.

Hal scratched his head. "I don't know, but surely she has to eat. Wish I had a carrot," he said.

"I could find some eggs," said the duck. "Eggs that are lost on the forest floor. I'll bet I could find four . . . or even more."

"Wait," said Madeline with a look of fright. "This is the forest where the tiger roams, and Daddy said he roams tonight."

The bunny shuddered. "The tiger? The tiger? The tiger's near?"

"I don't like tigers," Dasper said. "I hear they're mean."

"I'm afraid of tigers," Madeline said. "Oh, I wish I were home in bed."

"We need to make a plan," Hal said. "Maybe we'll stay strong if we sing a song."

Together the animals sang a happy song.

A wiggle and a squiggle and a giggle and a fiddle-ee-crew.

A quackle and a crackle and a chuckle and a riddle-ee-zoo.

A wiggle and a squiggle and a giggle.
A quackle and a crackle and a chuckle
and a fiddle-ee, riddle-ee-crew."

"I feel better," all three said together.

Madeline scratched her chin. "I can make a fire.
Tigers are afraid of fire."

Hal tried to look brave.

"Madeline, you gather sticks to make a fire.

Dasper, you gather eggs to eat,

and I'll stay with Audrey to keep her safe."

Dasper waddled off on his short little legs to find some eggs.
Madeline went along still singing their song.

When Dasper and Madeline had gone to gather eggs and sticks, Hal's nose began to twitch. Strange scents were in the air, and he began to fear.

He made a mattress of leaves for Audrey's bed and sat down beside her head. "I'll protect you and keep you safe," he said.

After the little angel fell asleep, Hal heard a roar. He trembled remembering what Madeline said.

Was it true?

Did the tiger roam tonight?

He looked up, down, and all around. He listened with his ears, and he was filled with fear.

The smell of danger grew stronger.

Hal heard another roar.

Was this the tiger that roamed at night?

Should Hal run?

Or stay and fight?

Stay and fight?

Hal knew that bunnies are too small.

Bunnies can't fight tigers at all.

Tigers are scary and big.

But bunnies are fast.

They can find holes to dig.

Hal looked at the little angel fast asleep on her bed, her blonde curls swirled around her head. The tiger would hurt her if he deserted her. She was so good. And she was from God. Hal couldn't run. It would be wrong. He had to stay. He had to be strong . . . he had to pray.

Then Hal heard footsteps crashing through the trees, heavy footsteps coming near.

Hal moaned and was filled with fear.

Was this the tiger that roamed at night?

Should he dash away and hide?

He spied two yellow eyes and heard a growl.

No time to think, just time to act, and Hal was fast.

He climbed on the mattress of leaves, covering the little angel by stretching himself over her to hide her. He put his rabbit ears together and fluffed them out long and made them wider. He lay very still and prayed.

Audrey the angel woke up from her deep, deep sleep.

"Was that a growl?" she cried. "Is that the tiger on the prowl? Oh, run little Hal and save yourself before the tiger eats you up."

"If I run, he'll eat you up. You're so good, and I'm just a naughty bunny, playing with my brothers, stealing carrots, and thinking of my tummy."

"No, I won't let you die for me. You must go and go soon."

The tiger stepped into the light of the moon.

He stopped and stood and stared.

He bared his teeth and roared again. He looked at Hal.

Hal didn't move and prayed with all his might.

This was indeed the tiger that roamed at night.

And then the tiger POUNCED.

With a burst of strength the angel cried out with all her might.
"Oh, Father God, please don't let the rabbit die for me!"

Her voice rose through the trees, up to the skies,
past the clouds, and into the starry night.

Suddenly, there was a flash of blinding light.

The tiger shrieked in fear and backed away. He turned and raced into the night,

deep into the forest

and out of sight.

As the light began to dim, another angel appeared.
She was tall and beautiful and stood beside the little angel's bed.

Audrey got up and looked around. She shook her head and her blonde curls bobbed up and down. "I feel fine now," she said.

"Why do you think that is?" the grown-up angel asked.

Audrey lowered her wings. "Because I remembered to pray. Prayer is what makes me strong. You teach me that every day."

She flapped her wings and gave a little jump.

"God wasn't too busy!" She spun around and her feet rose from the ground.

"He's never too busy. He was watching me all along just like He always watches everyone."

"Especially on this Easter day," the older angel said.

Just then the monkey and the duck came along. Dasper fluffed his tail and held out a basket of eggs.

Madeline patted the bow on top. "I made the basket out of sticks," she said, "just so you know."

The grown up angel smiled at them.

"And now . . ." she said to Audrey,

"I'm taking you back where you belong.

"Hal, you are Hallelujah Bunny, a good name indeed. You'll be the Easter Bunny, it's now decreed. You loved someone else better than yourself. Instead of running away, you put away your fears to stay and pray. You saved Audrey Angel's life today."

"Hallelujah! Yippee! I'd like to be the Easter Bunny," said Hal.

Audrey smiled and kissed Hal's cheek. He blushed and folded back his ears and stared up at the moon that shown as bright as the sun at noon.

The grown-up angel smiled at Hal and pointed to the moon. "Would you like to take a trip up there?"

Hal's big eyes began to stare. "Me?"

"Do you dare?"

"Yes!" Hal hopped around and wiggled his tail. "Do I get to see the moon? I've always wanted to go to the moon. How long will I get to stay up there?"

She pointed into the starry night.

"Whenever the moon is full and bright, you can be the Easter Bunny on the moon. You can stay as long as you like.

"So now every Easter when the moon is full, children will see a little bunny still, praying that children remember God loves them and always will.

"And every Easter morning a bunny brings to girls and boys a basket of eggs."

The beautiful angel then said, "Here we go!" They waved to the monkey and duck and rose from the ground,

higher and higher through the sky above,

up to the big, round moon

that shone as bright as the sun at noon.

"Now every spring when the moon is full, we can plainly see a bunny on the moon on Easter eve," said Nana.

"Wow! The Easter Bunny is a hero," said Christian.

"Yes!" said Ryan, Travis and Carson. "And that's how he got on the moon!"

YES, THERE REALLY IS A BUNNY ON THE MOON

If you look very carefully at a full moon you can see a bunny in the shadows on the west side. His ears are at the top. In the shadows on the left side of the moon, you might see a large bunny facing left with his ears back and an Easter egg at his feet like the picture in this book. Or you might see a bunny facing right with his ears flopped over and his head bowed as though he is praying. Or you might spot a smaller bunny at the top. Some people think the smaller bunny looks like he has his ears back and paws up praying. Others think it looks like he is racing over the top of the moon. Which rabbit do you see?

In many other parts of the world—especially Asia—people talk more about the "rabbit in the moon" than the man in the moon. Many stories and legends about the "rabbit in the moon" have been written in countries such as India, China, Japan, Korea and Mexico. These are stories about a brave rabbit that was rewarded and honored for his courage and can now be seen on the moon.

For those of us who celebrate Easter, the bunny in the moon is particularly significant because he tells us when Easter will take place every year. Although most holidays always come on the same day or at the same time of the month, Easter is sometimes in April and other times in March.

Do you know why that is?

It's because Easter always comes on a Sunday in spring after the first full moon appears. Spring begins on March 20. So if the full moon comes early, Easter might take place in March. But if the full moon appears in April, Easter comes later.

And do you know who is on the moon? It's the Easter Bunny just waiting for his special day. Once spring begins we can start looking for the first full moon. When we see it, we know the Easter Bunny is coming on the very next Sunday.

The Easter Bunny brings lots of fun to us at Easter, but there's more to the story. In our make-believe story the Easter Bunny was willing to sacrifice himself to save the angel. An even bigger and better story took place on the first real Easter. Visit bunnysideofeaster.com to read more about it.

Have a Happy Easter,

Linda Rooks

For parents, teachers and grandparents who want to go deeper with their children, you can visit my website at bunnysideofeaster.com for study questions that explore the deeper significances of Easter as related to the story you just read. Also, you will find games, more stories about the characters, further information about the moon and its legends, and more.